1st Grade

Invitations to Personal Reading
Curriculum Foundation Classroom Library
Scott, Foresman and Company

Books to Read Aloud	
The Big Golden Book of Poetry	edited by Jane Werner
Finders Keepers	Will and Nicolas
Little Frightened Tiger	Golden MacDonald
The Man Who Didn't Wash His Dishes	Phyllis Krasilovsky
The Old Woman and Her Pig	illustrated by Paul Galdone
Rosa-Too-Little	Sue Felt
Six Foolish Fishermen	retold by Benjamin Elkin
The Three Billy Goats Gruff	P. C. Asbjørnsen and J. E. Moe
Umbrella	Taro Yashima
Where Does the Butterfly Go When It Rains	May Garelick
Books to Enrich the Content Fields	
The Big Book of Real Fire Engines	illustrated by George Zaffo
The Listening Walk	Paul Showers
One Snail and Me	Emilie McLeod
The Sky Was Blue	Charlotte Zolotow
What Is A Turtle	Gene Darby
Books for Independent Reading	
Belling the Cat and Other Stories	retold by Leland Jacobs
Big Talk	Miriam Schlein
Cowboy Small	Lois Lenski
Gertie the Duck	Nicholas Georgiady and Louis Romano
Indian Two Feet and His Horse	Margaret Friskey
Josie and the Snow	Helen Buckley
Karen's Opposites	A. and M. Provensen
Millions and Millions and Millions!	Louis Slobodkin
Nothing but Cats, Cats, Cats	Grace Skaar
Robins and Rabbits	John Hawkinson

BIG TALK

This edition is printed and distributed by Scott, Foresman and Company by special arrangement with William R. Scott, Inc., New York, N.Y.

By Miriam Schlein

WITH ILLUSTRATIONS BY

Harvey Weiss

PUBLISHED BY

William R. Scott Inc., New York

Special Scott, Foresman and Company Edition
for the *Invitations to Personal Reading* Program

 LIBRARY OF CONGRESS CATALOG CARD NO. 55-6611

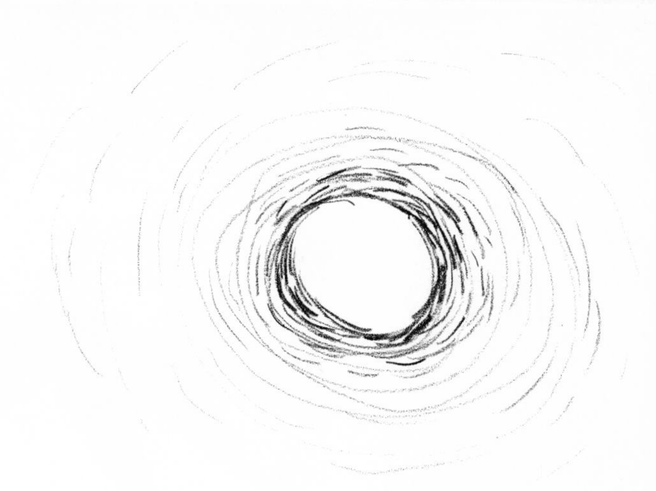

A little kangaroo and a big kangaroo
were holding a conversation.

"How high can you jump?"
asked the big kangaroo.

"I can jump as high as the sun," said the little one.

"How fast can you run?"
asked the big kangaroo.

"I can run as fast as the wind,"
said the little one.

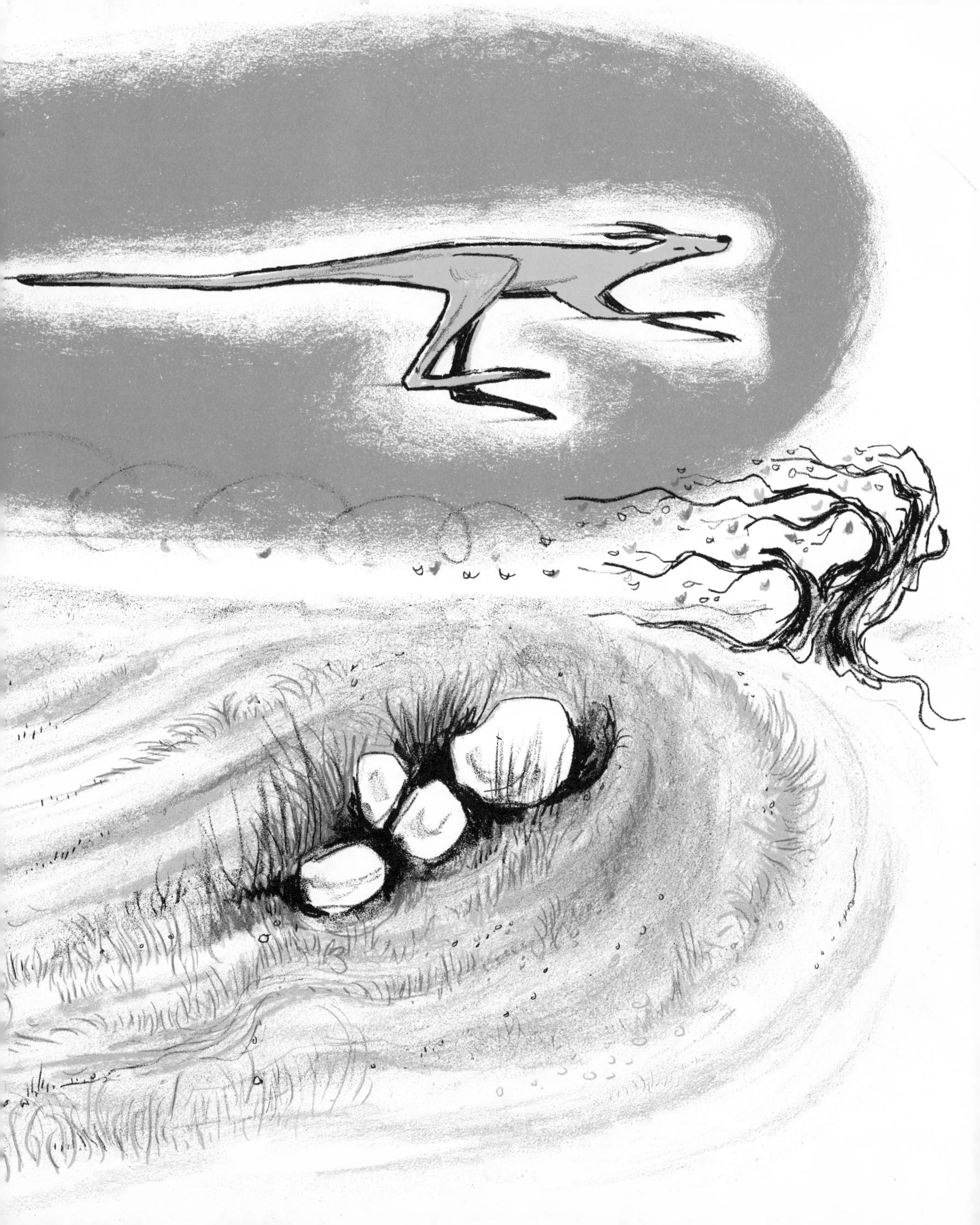

"How much can you drink?"

"I can drink up the sea."

"How much can you eat?"

"All the grass in the world."

"Are you brave?"

"As a lion."

"Are you tall?"

"As a tree!"

"Have you a funny face?"

"Ah," said the little kangaroo.
"My face is as funny as a kookaburra
and a koala bear
dancing in the moonlight!"

"Oh," said the big kangaroo.
"I'm glad you told me that.
Because, with all those other things
you told me, I wasn't sure.
But now I *know*
you're my own little kangaroo.
Hop in."

The little kangaroo
hopped into the pouch.

"But you will," said his mother.

The little kangaroo peeked up.
"Will what?"

"Will be brave as a lion,
and grow tall as a tree,
and jump high as the sun,
and run fast as the wind."

"Will I *really*?" asked the little kangaroo.

"Oh, yes," said his mother, "I know."

"Ah," said the little one, sleepily.
"I'm glad you told me that.
Because, you know, *I* really wasn't so sure
about all those things myself!"

OTHER YOUNG SCOTT BOOKS BY

Miriam Schlein

THE FOUR LITTLE FOXES

WHEN WILL THE WORLD BE MINE?

ELEPHANT HERD

GO WITH THE SUN

SHAPES

FAST IS NOT A LADYBUG

HEAVY IS A HIPPOPOTAMUS